D0131341

NIGHT CIRCUS

 Designed by Rita Marshall Published in 2015 by Creative Editions
P.O. Box 227, Mankato, MN 56002 USA Creative Editions is an imprint of The Creative Company www.thecreativecompany.us

Printed in China Library of Congress Cataloging-in-Publication Data Delessert, Etienne, author, illustrator. Night circus / by Etienne Delessert; illustrated by Etienne Delessert. Summary: Artist Etienne Delessert reflects on his lifelong pursuit of art using the dreamlike scenario of a circus procession filled with fairy-tale allusions and literary inspirations. ISBN 978-1-56846-277-6 1. Delessert, Etienne—Juvenile literature. 2. Illustrators—Switzerland—Biography—Juvenile literature. 3. Fantasy in art—Juvenile literature. I. Title.
NC988.5.D45A2 2015 741.6092—dc23 [B] 2014022711

First edition 9 8 7 6 5 4 3 2 1

NIGHT CIRCUS

etienne delessert

Creative Editions

On a calm September evening,
I was walking my dog along Route 44
when headlights flashed in front of me.

My cat Pluto was driving past in an antique racing car,

slowly pulling ten old-fashioned wooden flatbeds.

On the first car were three clowns named Franz, Sam, and Eugène.
They asked:

"My friend, do you read poetry?"

{The writers Franz Kafka, Samuel Beckett, and Eugène Ionesco}

On the second stage, a pack of mad dogs howled off-key.
One of them smirked:

"Do you hear our music?"

Next came a group of angels, gathered around a chess game:

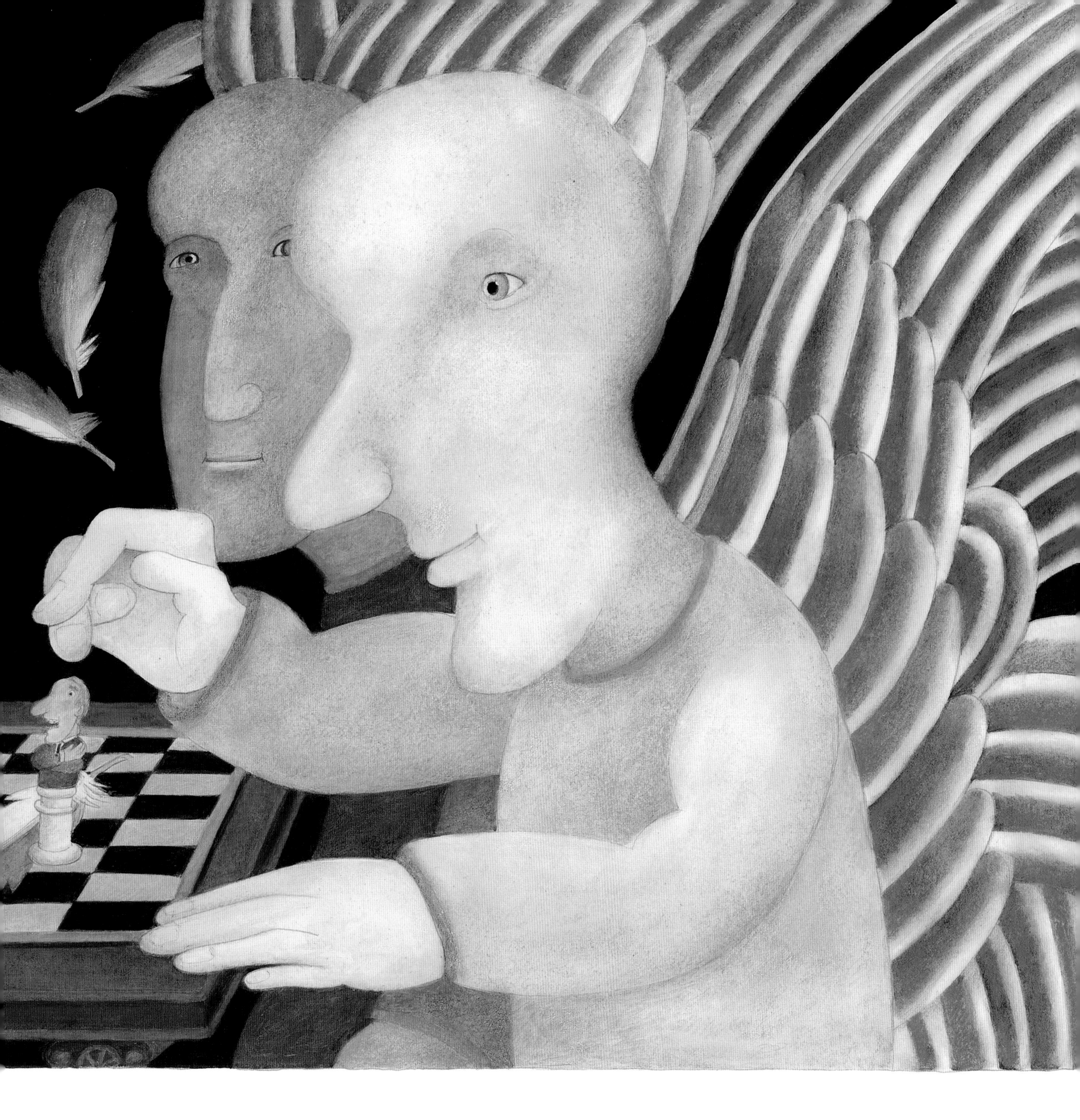

"Want to play with us?"

Then a lion jumped through a ring of fire:

"Can you feel the heat?"

A troupe of juggling acrobats rolled past on the next car.
One of them turned toward me:

"Do you know this word?"

On the sixth stage, a black swan hissed at a group of pesky dwarfs:

"Could you please tell them to stop plucking me?"

Three little pigs sliced a large wolf pie as their car clunked down the road:

"Do you want a piece of pie?"

As she painted the claws of a giant alligator,
a little girl in a red hat smiled:

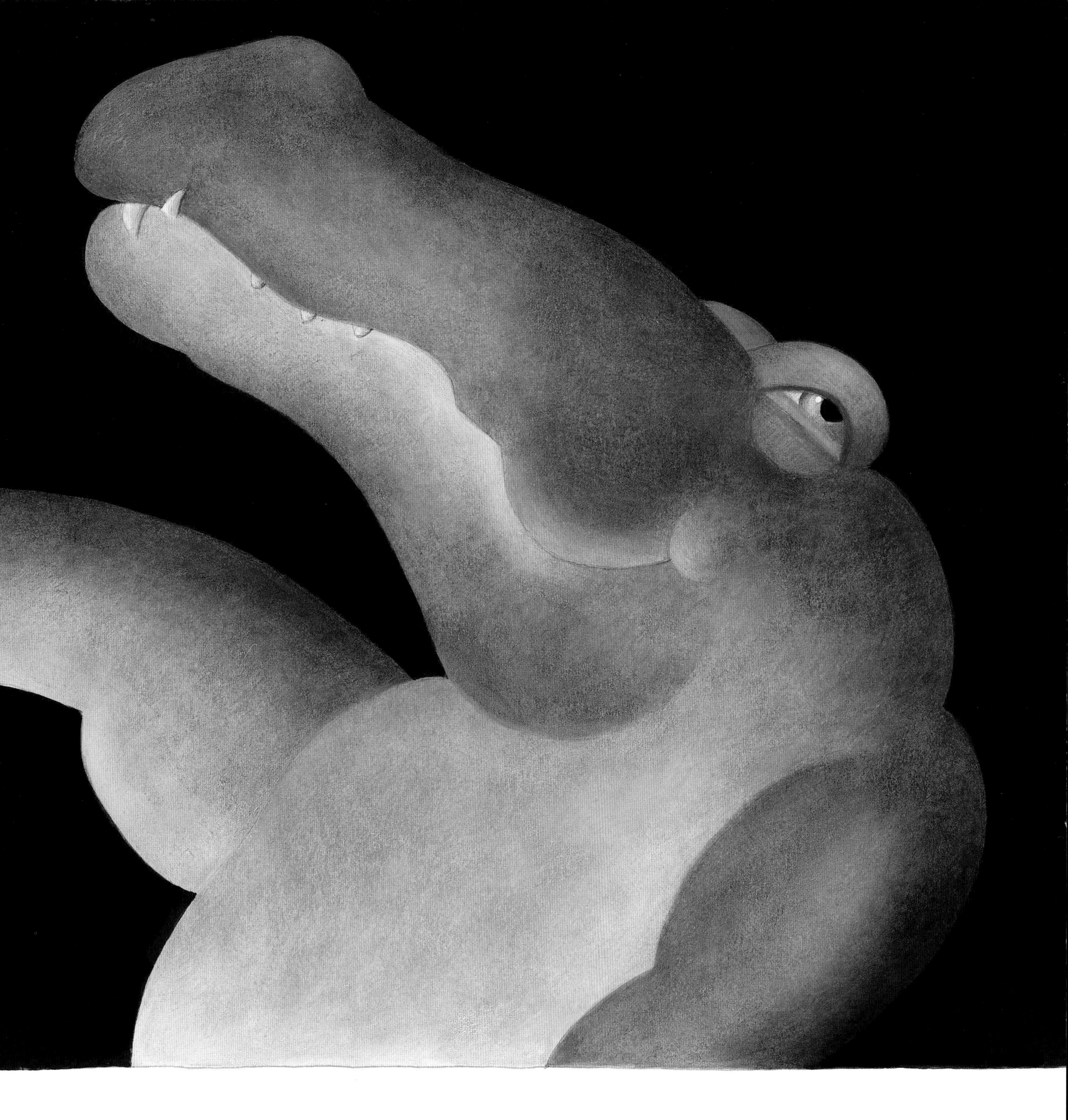

"Would you choose a better color?"

On the ninth stage, a fiddler played an ole time Bluegrass tune.

"Do you remember this song?"

On the last flatbed sat a large snow globe
with a million butterflies, all aflutter.

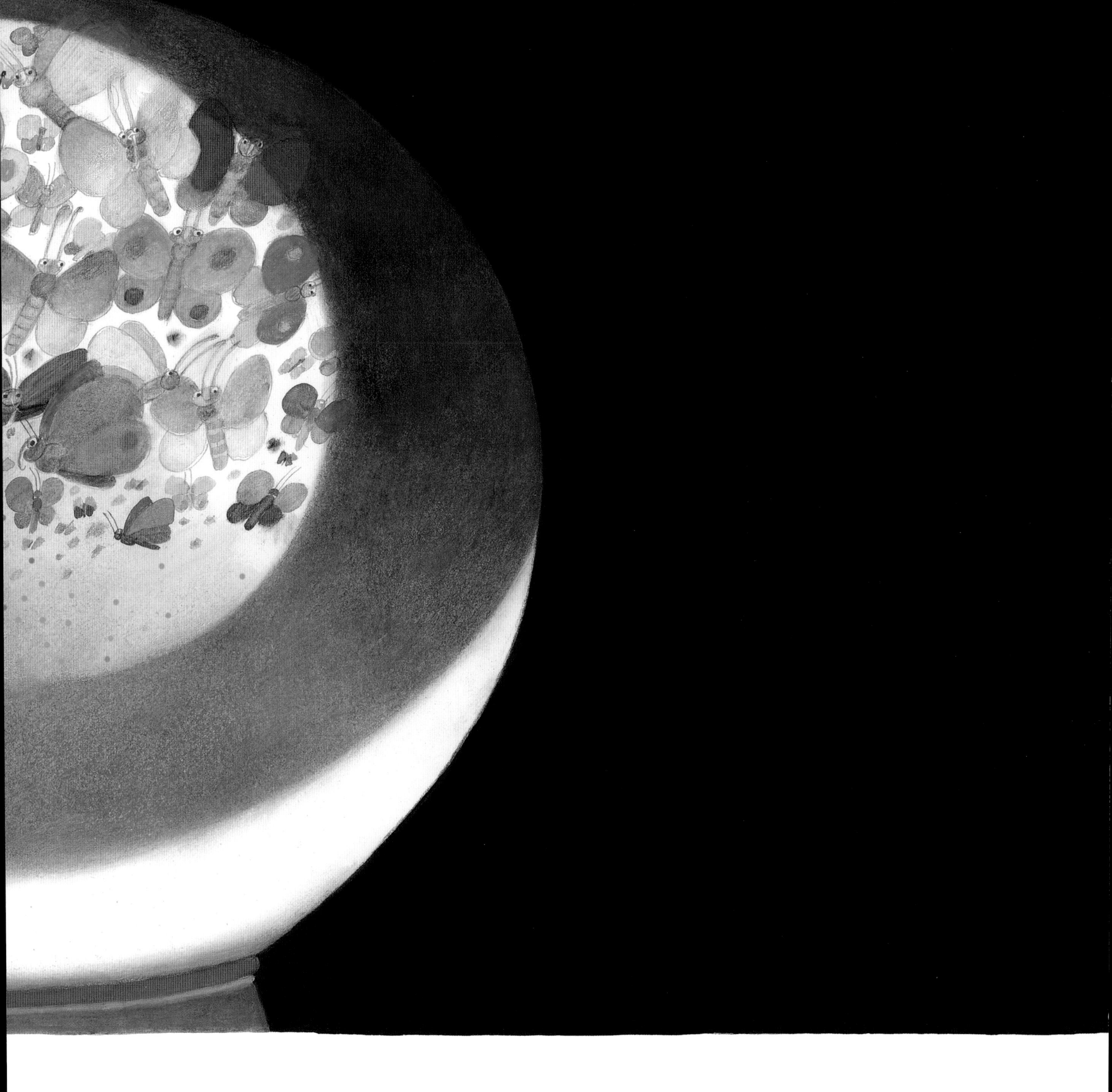

I couldn't hear a sound.

I watched as the caravan was swallowed in a warm, soft light.

I held my dog tight as we followed behind.

We all moved slowly toward a finely chiseled desert mirage.
Someone asked:

"Want to play now?…"

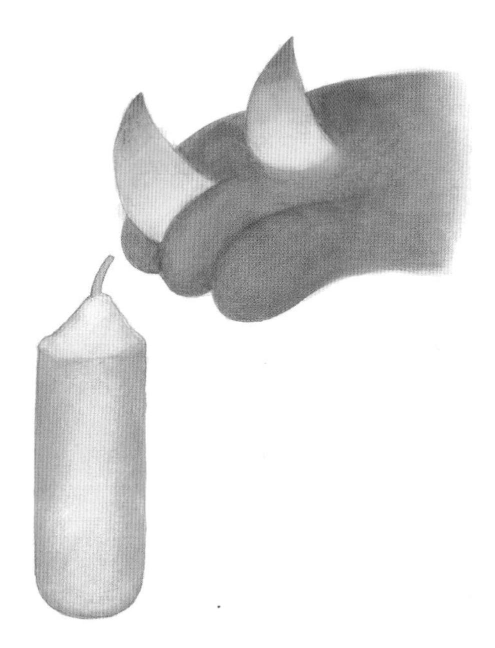

I approached the lion and his ring of fire.
We lit a candle.

It was my night circus!